ERYN

GW00728002

Crabapple End

Can you keep a secret? You can? GOOD.

This book will share with you the secrets of some special little animals called teezles who are so clever they could almost be called magic.

These happy little creatures live in Crabapple Wood, where they build their underground homes beneath large trees. They get their surnames from the tree under which they live.

They live in peace with all other animals, insects and birds and help them when they are injured, sick or in need.

Although teezles use nature's gifts in many wonderful ways, they always protect and preserve the countryside.

So! If you are good and kind and always care for the wonderful things that life gives to us then, maybe one day, you could become a friend of the teezles.

"GO JOYFULLY" THROUGH LIFE

THE TEEZLES
and the
DEER'S DILEMMA

by Terry Barber

Published by Peter Haddock Limited,
Bridlington, England.

© Terry Barber

Illustrated by Wizard Art,
courtesy of Bernard Thornton Artists, London.

THE TEEZLES and the DEER'S DILEMMA

One lovely spring morning Wren Elm and her best friend, Fragrance Holly, were gathering herbs when they heard the sound of sobbing. They moved a large fern to one side and gasped in surprise. There, lying very still, was a beautiful baby deer. The fawn looked very frightened and had tears in its big, brown eyes. "Don't be frightened: we won't hurt you," said Wren gently. "Why are you crying?"

"I have lost my mummy and I am very hungry," sobbed the fawn.

"Where is your mummy?" asked Fragrance.

"She went looking for food two sunrises ago and she hasn't come back, so I don't know what to do," whispered the fawn.

"First, we will take you home and get you some food. Then, we will find your mother," said Wren.

"My mother told me to stay here. If she returns she won't know where I am," replied the fawn.

"Don't worry, I will stay here in case she returns," said Fragrance.

Wren led the fawn back home and explained the deer's dilemma to the other teezles. Silk Oak brought a bowl of clover milk which the baby deer lapped up greedily.

Linden Beech announced that not only the teezles but all the animals and birds in Crabapple Wood would be asked to search for the female deer. Every inch of the wood was searched and the birds flew far and wide, but not a trace of the missing doe was found.

It was nearly nightfall when the barn owl flew into the wood. "I have found the deer you are looking for," squawked the owl. "I was asleep all day as usual but, when I woke, there in the barn was the doe."

"Is she unharmed?" asked Wren anxiously.

"Yes, but she is very worried about her baby and says that the farmer intends to take her to a zoo in the morning," the owl answered.

"What is a zoo?" asked young Clumsy Tub.

"It is a place where man animals imprison wild animals in cages," explained Linden Beech gravely, "but we can't allow that to happen to Mrs Deer. We must rescue her tonight."

A small rescue party was formed. Fern Oak decided to fly back on the owl to the farm to reassure the captive deer and make plans for the rescue before the others arrived.

When they landed on the roof of the barn it was nearly dark.

"The farmer should be asleep before the others get here," whispered the owl, "but make no noise because the vicious farm dog will bark at the slightest sound."

The owl took Fern inside the barn and carried him down on to a bale of straw near the captive deer. Fern explained to her that her baby was safe and that soon she herself would be free.

"How will you get the door open?" asked the deer.

"Don't worry, we will find a way," grunted Fern, as he squeezed through a hole at the bottom of the door.

When the other teezles arrived the moon was shining brightly. Fern led them to the barn door. "I have found this," he whispered, picking up a long cane. "We must try to push the peg out of the latch with it."

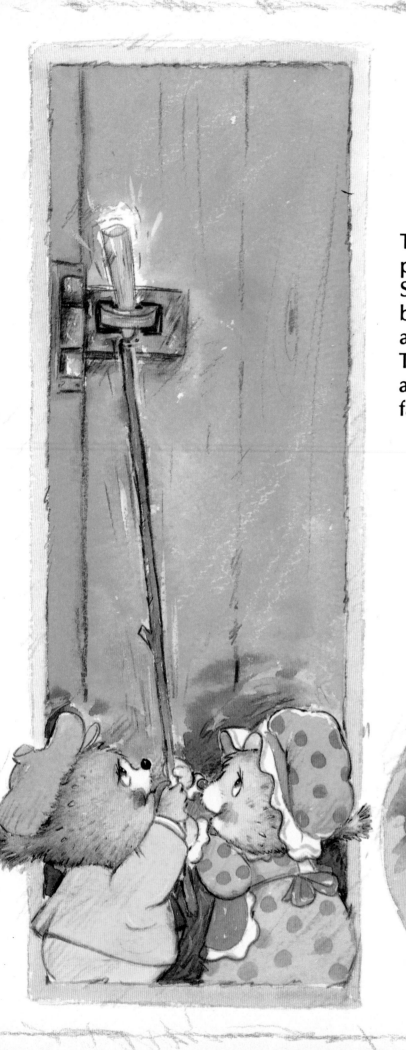

They lifted the cane and pushed with all their might. Suddenly, out popped the peg but, unfortunately, it fell into a bucket with a loud clatter. The dog started to bark loudly and the lights in the farmhouse came on.

The teezles pulled open the barn door. At the same time the farmhouse door also opened and out bounded the dog, followed by the farmer carrying a shotgun.

"Run for your life," cried Fragrance to the deer and the frightened animal fled towards the wood. The farmer aimed his gun at the deer but, before he could fire, the barn owl swooped down with a fearsome shriek and knocked the gun from his hand. The terrified farmer staggered back and fell full-length into the horse trough.

Meanwhile, the teezles had jumped into a wheelbarrow to hide but the dog had spotted them. As its head appeared over the edge of the wheelbarrow, Silk Oak was prepared. She threw the contents of the pouch she carried into the dog's face. It was teezle pepper.

As the dog stood sneezing and the farmer sat freezing, the teezles headed home to the joyful reunion of the baby deer with its mother.

FAMILY QUEST

Take a walk and see how many birds you can identify.

FAMILY QUESTION

What colour are the eggs of a barn owl?

If you don't know, go to your local library and look for a book to help you find out.